MW01010082

FOREST CHILD

FOREST CHILD

BY MARNI MᶜGEE • ILLUSTRATED BY A. SCOTT BANFILL

GREEN TIGER PRESS

PUBLISHED BY SIMON & SCHUSTER

NEW YORK LONDON TORONTO SYDNEY TOKYO SINGAPORE

GREEN TIGER PRESS
1230 Avenue of the Americas
New York, New York 10020
Text copyright © 1994 by Marni McGee
Illustrations copyright © 1994 by A. Scott Banfill
All rights reserved including the right of reproduction
in whole or in part in any form.
GREEN TIGER PRESS and colophon are trademarks of Simon & Schuster.
The text for this book is set in 21-point
Stempel Schneidler. The illustrations were done in acrylics.
Manufactured in the United States of America

10   9   8   7   6   5   4   3

Library of Congress Cataloging-in-Publication Data
McGee, Marni. Forest child / by Marni McGee ;
illustrated by A. Scott Banfill. p. cm.
Summary: A child lost in the forest is fed
and protected by the animals there.
[1. Forest animals—Fiction. 2. Lost children—Fiction.]
I. Banfill, A. Scott, ill. II. Title.
PZ7.M478463Fo 1994 [E]—dc20 92-37148 CIP AC
ISBN: 0-671-86608-7

For my son, Claude, with love,
and in memory of James Butler McGee, Jr.
—M.M.

To the memory of Grandpa Bard
—A.S.B.

The sleepy sun began to slide
down the rosy curve of sky;
and as her light turned to gold,
a child came into the forest alone.

Hearing the sound of a stranger,
the owl awoke and blinked its eyes.
"Whoo," it asked, "are you?"
But the child did not tell his name.
"I'm lost," he cried.
"Won't someone help me
find my way home?"

The owl hooted in reply,
"You must leave the forest. Go!
Humans come only
to catch and kill us,
and you are one of them.
You must go, go away!"

A harsh, cold wind began to blow.
The forest itself came alive with sounds —
mumbling, grumbling, growling low.
The child shivered.
All around him,
dark, unblinking eyes
watched through a curtain of trees.
He must run —
but where,
where could he go?

Suddenly, from deep in the forest,
the child heard a cry.
He stood still and listened.
Someone was calling for help —
but who?
The child began to run.
On quick, bare feet, he
followed the sound until
he reached the brook.

Near the water's edge,
he saw a rabbit,
caught in a hunter's trap.
The child knelt down.
"Don't be afraid," he crooned.
"Be still. Soon, soon you'll be free."
Gently, the child pulled apart
the prongs that held the rabbit captive.

The rabbit shook itself;
and as it quickly hopped away,
the mumbling, grumbling,
growling stopped.
The harsh, cold wind grew still,
and a hush fell over the forest.
The child held his breath —
looked up.
All around him were animals,
creatures of every kind,
forming a circle of feather and fur.
No longer fierce and glaring,
now their eyes were kind.

"Don't be afraid," said the wolf.
"We will not harm you,
   for you have become one of us."

"Yes," said the brook, "indeed!
Won't you come in for a swim?
I'll wash your face and cool your feet."
The child jumped in.
A family of fish swam by his side.
A turtle tickled his toes.
The child paddled and splashed about
until he saw that the sky
had changed from gold to gray.

His eyes grew wide.
"It's dark," he said. "I've got to get home!
  I know that my mother will worry."
"Whoo," said the kindly owl,
"will guide the child?
  Whoo will help him find
  the way home?"
"I will," declared the eagle.
"My eyes are keen. But the journey
  is long. The child has wandered far.
  Tonight he must stay here with us.
  At dawn, I will lead him home."

"Whoo then," said the owl,
"will carry a message
  to say that the child is safe?"
"I will," said the dove. "Let me.
  My wings are swift; my voice is sweet.
  I'll fly to those who love the child
  and tell them he is safe."

"Very well," said the owl,
"but the child will need his supper soon.
 Whoo will give him something to eat?"
"Let me," said the bear. "Let me!
 I'll share the ripe, red berries
 that grow on prickly vines
 and the honey hidden
 in the hollows of trees."
"And I," said the squirrel, flicking its tail,
"will show him where to find some seeds,
 sweet and good to eat."

After the child had eaten
all that he could eat,
the kindly owl asked,
"Whoo will play with the child
until it's time to go to sleep?"
"Let me," said a deer with velvet eyes.
"I'll run with him. We'll race.
And when he's tired, I'll let him ride —
his arms around my neck."
The deer and the child romped and ran
until the sky grew dark.

"Whoo," said the owl very softly,
"whoo now will give the child some light,
  for he's a stranger in our wood."
"Let us," said the moon and stars together.
"We'll shine our light through forest leaves
  and chase the shadows away."

The owl nodded, rustling its wings.
"And whoo will make a bed?
 Soon the child will need to sleep —
 already his eyelids are drooping."
"Please," said the rabbit, "let me!
 I'll gather flowers and bits of grass.
 I'll weave a mat beneath the oak
 with pillows made from moss."

"Yes," said the owl, "very well.
And whoo will keep watch with me
till morning summons the sun?"
"Let me," said the wolf. "I'll help,
for you are wise and I am strong.
Together we'll stand guard.
The child will know that he is safe."
And so the child lay down to rest.
The moon and stars cast patterns
of light all around him.
The animals gathered close around.
Each one said, "Good night."

"Whoo," said the owl, whispering now,
"whoo will sing a lullaby?"
"No need, no need," the nightingale trilled.
"Our precious child is fast asleep."